Photo
Perfect

GIRLS ONLY (GO!)

Dreams on Ice
Only the Best
A Perfect Match
Reach for the Stars
Follow the Dream
Better Than Best
Photo Perfect

GIRLS GO ONLY!

7

Photo Perfect

BEVERLY LEWIS

BETHANY HOUSE PUBLISHERS
MINNEAPOLIS, MINNESOTA 55438

Published by Bethany House Publishers
A Ministry of Bethany Fellowship International
11400 Hampshire Avenue South
Bloomington, Minnesota 55438
www.bethanyhouse.com

Printed in the United States of America by
Bethany Press International, Bloomington, Minnesota 55438

Library of Congress Cataloging-in-Publication Data

Lewis, Beverly, 1949-
    Photo perfect / by Beverly Lewis.
        p.   cm. — (Girls only (GO!) ; 7)
Summary: Heather becomes obsessed with losing weight after her
brother falls lifting her during ice skating practice.
    ISBN 1-55661-642-2 (pbk.)
    [1. Weight control—Fiction. 2. Ice skating—Fiction. 3. Brothers
and sisters—Fiction. 4. Christian life—Fiction.] I. Title. II. Series.
    PZ7.L58464 Ph   2001
[Fic]—dc21   2001001325

To
Janell Hall,
a faithful fan (and homeschooler!)
in Fortson, Georgia.

AUTHOR'S NOTE

I wish to thank my daughter Julie for her help with the modeling-agency scene in this book. Thanks so much, honey!

Also, my great appreciation to the U.S. Figure Skating Association and the International Skating Union (*http://www.usfsa.org* and *http://www.isu.org* for additional information about ice dancing and free skating).

BEVERLY LEWIS is the bestselling author of over sixty books, including the popular CUL-DE-SAC KIDS and SUMMERHILL SECRETS series, as well as her adult fiction series, THE HERITAGE OF LANCASTER COUNTY, and *The Postcard* and its sequel, *The Crossroad*. Her picture books include *Cows in the House*, a rollicking Thai folktale for all ages, and *Annika's Secret Wish*, a Swedish story set in the nineteenth century. Bev, her husband, and their three children make their home in Colorado, within miles of the Olympic Training Center, headquarters of the U.S. Olympic Committee.

 CHAPTER *1*

It all started at Dottie Forster's Boutique, situated across from the skating rink in Alpine Lake's shopping mall. Heather Bock sat waiting for her mother, who was getting another one of her funky, too-curly perms. Eager to pass the time, Heather reached for a teen magazine and began paging through until she came to the fashion and trends section. Her gaze zeroed in on an article titled, "Pin Thin: The Stick Clique."

She peered closely at the young and glamorous models featured on the two-page spread. "Wow, that *is* skinny," she whispered.

"What's up?" asked Mom from the beautician's chair.

"Oh, it's just these pencil-thin jeans," she replied, absorbed in the new spring styles. "I think it's time *I* get some new clothes."

"Well, save your pennies," Dottie Forster piped up from her salon cabinet, where hair-color concoctions and clean combs and brushes were stored. "That's what *my* mother always used to say."

Yeah . . . back during the Great Depression, thought Heather, dismissing the beautician's offhanded remark.

But the mental picture of tall and super-lean girls smiling back from the pages of the fashion magazine stayed with Heather the rest of the day. Even as she dusted and vacuumed her bedroom, and later worked at her computer, doing research for a homeschool project, thoughts of the ultra-thin models lingered in her mind.

Writing the final paragraphs of her paper, Heather stopped for a moment and stared up at her poster of world-renowned British ice dancers, Olympic stars Torvill and Dean. She daydreamed about her own athletic goals, well within reach. With every ounce of zip and vigor, she longed to be a skating sensation, right along with her older brother and ice-dancing partner, Kevin, who was just as blond and nearly as focused. No, he was as *equally* caught up in the sport as she.

Sometimes, though, she convinced herself that between the two of them, *she* was the skater most eager for Olympic gold. The sound of boisterous applause thrilled her, as well as the unmistakable echo of the loudspeaker broadcasting her name—with Kevin's, of course.

Finished with her assignment—the history of the Olympics—she stood and stretched at her desk. Then, turning toward her calendar, she flipped it to the month of July, counting the weeks and months until the next big skate contest. She circled the second Saturday and wrote in big letters: *Summer Ice Spectacular*.

Only four more months. If she and Kevin could land a first-place medal for that event, they'd have a good shot at the Junior Olympics. She hugged herself, ready to take on the world of ice dancing.

Joanne, Heather's six-year-old adopted sister, came in without knocking. The chubby brunette sat down hard on Heather's bed, her feet dangling. "Can you help me?"

"With what?" Heather went and sprawled out on the bed, waiting to hear what Joanne had to say. "What's spinning around in your little head tonight?"

"Nothin's spinning," came the quick reply. "And my head's not little!"

"Oh, really?"

"Yep, and besides, I've been thinking that it's time I start getting in shape."

"For what?"

Her sister's eyes were playful. "You know, in case I decide to go out for something like . . ." She stopped for a second, then continued. "Something like ice hockey or maybe even Alpine skiing, like your friend Miranda."

Heather didn't dare laugh. Even though Joanne's eyes

twinkled with mischief, Heather wasn't sure just how serious her sis was. "Have you been thinking about this for a long time?"

Joanne's head bobbed up and down. "Oh yes. I want to build up my muscle tone, start doing more sit-ups every day. Like Mommy does with her workout DVD."

"That's nice."

"No, really . . . I *want* to be a healthy vessel for God."

Heather let a tiny laugh slip past her lips. This was too much. "Don't you mean a *willing* vessel?"

"Sure . . . that, too." Joanne jumped off the bed and bounced toward the door, her long hair hanging loose around her shoulders. "So . . . will you help me?"

She had no idea where this conversation was headed. "What do you want me to do?"

"Help me get rid of my flabby muscles." Joanne pointed to her upper arms.

"You've got to be kidding." Heather eyed her sister. Slightly plump around the middle, but lots of six-year-olds had little or no waistline. Nothing to worry about. "You're fine, Joanne. Kids your age are supposed to be chubby. Besides, when you grow a bit taller in a few years, you'll slim right down."

"But I don't want to wait." Abruptly, Joanne turned and left the room.

What's that about? wondered Heather, reaching for her teen devotional Bible.

Morning training sessions came very early in the Bock

household. Both she and Kevin had a long day tomorrow, and Coach McDonald expected them to be prompt. After practice, they'd have to hurry home to shower, change clothes, and hit the books around the dining-room table, with Mom as their teacher. At the present time, one of their homeschool study units was personal hygiene and nutrition. Mom's idea, as usual. She was a stickler for eating healthy foods and, in general, taking good care of "God's property," as she liked to refer to her children's bodies.

Opening the pages to the devotional for the day, Heather was caught off guard. Surprised, really. The Scripture reading was 1 Timothy 4:8. "For physical training is of some value, but godliness has value for all things, holding promise for both the present life and the life to come."

She thought of Joanne's comments about wanting to get in shape. Had her sister been reading Heather's devotional book? Joanne was a good reader, advanced beyond her years, one of the benefits of being schooled at home—you didn't get stuck in a single grade level for a full year.

Hmm. She wondered about her suspicions. Not that Joanne was ever known to nose around in her big sister's bedroom. Mom was totally opposed to it. And the younger children—Joanne and Tommy, both—knew enough not to cross any of the clearly defined boundaries set up in the house. Joanne must have come up with the notion to work out entirely on her own.

Heather hurried to her dresser and picked up her brush, beginning her nightly ritual of brushing her shoulder-length hair twenty-five times on each side. As she did, she thought of the skinny-minny models she'd seen in the magazine at Dottie Forster's Boutique. Did they exercise vigorously to look that skeletal, or did they go without eating? And what would cause a girl to want to starve herself that way?

CHAPTER 2

Heather flew through her day, dragging out of bed before dawn, dressing for practice. She breathed a prayer before rushing out the door with Mom and Kevin. "Help us meet our skating goals for today, dear Lord," she whispered.

"You're rehearsing your lifts today," Mom reminded them on the drive to the skating rink.

"I'm ready," Kevin said, grinning and proudly showing off his arm muscles. "I'm in great shape."

Mom nodded. "You're strong because you lift weights. Keep up the good work."

Kevin groaned. Lifting arm and leg weights wasn't his favorite thing to do, but it was essential to build and strengthen the upper torso, as well as a skater's legs.

"Thank goodness I'm still shorter than Kevin," added Heather.

"If you pass me up, maybe *you* can start doing the lifts, with me over your head," Kevin said, laughing.

"No, thanks," she replied.

When it came to lifts, there was no set rule that the guy had to be the one to lift the girl. Actually, a short girl lifting a taller partner would shock the judges. And no skater wanted to risk offending or upsetting a judge.

Heather was ready for anything today. Totally pumped and eager to work.

Mom pulled into the mall parking lot, pausing to look at each of them before opening the door. "I'm so proud of you both," she said. "You work so hard."

"Coach McDonald insists on it. We have no choice." Kevin grinned at Heather, his blue eyes shining.

"Okay, so let's get going." Heather opened the car door and raced her brother to the mall entrance.

Coach greeted them with a grin and a wave and sported a bright red tie. He always wore a pressed white dress shirt and a bright tie when coaching. His trademark.

To warm up—to avoid tearing muscles—both Heather and Kevin did their off-ice training, working on calf, thigh, and hip muscles, as well as spine, shoulders, and neck. Flexibility was important, the foundation of all aspects of skating. Stretching and bending three or four times a day, for several minutes at a time, was crucial to good skating—something

Coach McDonald had instilled in them. So was ballet class, which Heather took from dance instructor Natalie Johnston, along with three other Girls Only Club members.

Physical conditioning, the regular scheduled routine of exercise and repetitions, was their *protocol*. Heather and her brother trained this way without fail each day, except for one full rest day per week. In addition to that, one other training day was less of a workout day.

After the off-ice warm-ups, they laced up their skates and did some hard stroking on the ice, including high-speed skating. The stroking helped develop their upper-body strength. Holding arms at a level between the chest and waist, they skated separately for a full two and a half minutes, the time required for the short program.

"Judges like to watch for drooping arms," Coach McDonald reminded them, "especially toward the final seconds of a program."

Heather knew this to be true. Coach pounded away at certain things during each session. Practicing four days a week—every other weekend was spent training in Colorado Springs, at the Olympic Training Center—helped strengthen their late jumps and lessen the chance of fatigue happening in the upper body.

"Let's work on your lifts," Coach said, skating close to them. He followed them around the rink, spotting them, especially on the armpit lifts. Though they were the easiest group of overhead lifts, Coach liked to play it safe.

Today, Heather was going to practice something for the

first time. She would spring off the ice, into the armpit lift. Once Kevin's arms were completely extended and she was fully off the ice, he would lower her back to the ice, very gently, turning around while supporting her in midair.

Coach insisted on spotting her, even though she had done the less-advanced move with her hands resting on Kevin's shoulders. "You're absolutely ready for this," Coach said, guiding them through as he skated backward, facing them. "Think through each step, every move and turn."

They skated another half length down the ice. On cue, Heather sprang up and off the ice. Up . . . up she flew, resisting the urge to touch her brother's shoulders. Yes! She could do this without assurance of a prop. No crutches needed.

Easy.

Then it happened. While she was being lifted, scary as it already was, Kevin caught an edge and fell backward. Head forward, Heather saw the ice rushing to meet her. She reached out her hands to catch her fall, and when she did, her knee hit the ice. She cried out as searing pain shot through her knee.

Instantly, Coach was there. Kevin got up and brushed himself off, seemingly not hurt, only stunned by the sudden fall.

Heather sat on the ice, holding her knee, trying to rub the pain away. She'd trusted her brother. Yet, in spite of their long history, knowing each other's rhythm—in spite of that—she felt he'd let her down. Literally.

"I can't believe you dropped me, Kevin."

"It was an accident, and you know it."

She was crying now. "You . . . *hurt* me!"

Kevin muttered, "Well, if you weren't so heavy . . ."

"What did you say?" she shot back.

"Uh . . . forget it."

But she'd heard him. "You think I'm fat?" she spouted. "Is that it?"

Coach intervened. "Nobody's fat here. Things like this happen, even to the most experienced skaters." He inspected Heather's bruised knee. "I guess we'll have to call it a day. Have your doctor take a look, and stay off the leg for a couple of days."

"We won't be trying *that* lift anytime soon," Kevin said as Coach helped Heather off the rink.

"We'll see how she's doing next Monday," Coach said.

Mom was worried, as usual, assisting Heather with her skates, getting her safely to the car. "Don't worry, honey," Mom said. "You'll be as good as new."

Yeah, right, thought Heather, still upset.

What bothered her even more were Kevin's words on the ice: *"If you weren't so heavy."* "Maybe it's my partner who's got the problem," she whispered in the backseat.

Mom held her cell phone, waiting for the doctor's office. "What's that, dear?"

"Oh, nothing," Heather replied.

But it *was* something. She felt absolutely rotten. Being accused falsely like that was . . . well, she *knew* she wasn't too heavy for her brother to lift. Not when they had the right momentum. Not when she helped him by bounding off the ice, getting herself up in the air. Besides, he had done the move hundreds of times before. She refused to accept Kevin's heartless comment. There was no truth in it. None.

Stopping by the doctor's office took less than thirty minutes. "One of the benefits of living in a small town," Mom pointed out on the drive home.

Heather nursed her knee on the living-room sofa, keeping it iced and elevated. *Two days out of training is disaster*, she thought. Especially with the July skate event coming up in the near future. Kevin, of course, could carry on without her, keeping in shape and toned. Knowing him, he would, too. When it came to skating, nothing kept her brother down. Not even minor injuries.

Meanwhile, she read and wrote her homeschool assignments while lying down, following both the doctor's and Coach's orders. At midmorning break, Joanne and Tommy came to check on her. Typically, she would have been pleased with their thoughtful attention. But today, after what happened at the rink, she felt annoyed by their kindness and concern. "I'm fine," she snapped. "Don't baby me."

"Doesn't look like you're fine," Joanne said.

"Nope." Tommy stuck out his lower lip. "Your knee's real messed up."

She shooed them out of the living room. "Doesn't Mom need you in the kitchen?"

Tommy shook his head. "She wants us here, with you."

Thrilling. What she preferred was to be alone, sulking about the dreadful morning—Kevin's fall, his dropping her. The accident had spoiled everything.

CHAPTER 3

The members of the Girls Only Club met that afternoon. Jenna Song, team captain and award-winning gymnast, was their club president. Livvy Hudson, skater extraordinaire, was vice president. And Miranda Garcia, known as Manda, a first-class Alpine skier, was their newest member.

All three girls showed up at Heather's house after school. In the past, they'd met at Jenna's because her enormous bedroom was set up with a barre and a wall of mirrors on one side. The girls liked to do stretches, centerwork, and pointe technique together.

When the others had heard of Heather's bruised knee, though, they quickly changed the location.

Heather's mom was all for it. "We'll have fun serving frozen yogurt with fresh strawberries," she said, making a place for the girls at the kitchen table.

Joanne and Tommy pushed an extra chair up close to Heather, so she could prop up her leg. Then they scooted off, leaving the foursome snug in the large country kitchen. Mom closed the door behind her as she left.

"Wow," whispered Livvy, "this is really great of your mom."

"No kidding," Jenna said. "Be sure to thank her for us."

Miranda nodded. "Maybe we ought to rotate our club meeting locations."

Heather wondered what everyone thought of that. But nothing more was said, and no one moved to put it to a vote. The truth was, Jenna's remodeled attic bedroom was the ideal place for their meetings.

Livvy launched the touchy subject first. "How'd Kevin drop you?"

Momentarily, Heather relived the startling instant. "He caught an edge and went down backward. No fun."

"And you came crashing onto the ice?" Livvy asked, the one club member who could relate most.

"Let's put it this way: If I hadn't caught myself, my head might be in traction right now . . . or worse."

"Worse?" Jenna asked, her beautiful Korean eyes squinting nearly shut.

"Well, you know. . . ."

"No, *tell* us," Jenna prodded, and Miranda leaned on her elbows, scooting forward.

"Ever hear of a concussion?" she asked. "Not a good thing for a skater."

"Or *anyone*," said Manda, pulling on her dark hair. "Believe me, I know what I'm talking about."

"You had a concussion?" asked Heather.

Manda nodded. "Yes, and it's unbearable. Your head throbs, and you're totally out of it." She sighed. "The worst thing is everyone babies you because your skull and your brain collided."

"Thank goodness Heather doesn't have *that*." Jenna reached over and patted Heather's arm.

"Yeah," said Livvy softly.

Heather did not reveal the first thing out of Kevin's mouth after they'd fallen. She would say nothing about it—she could just hear her girl friends laugh. They were always telling her how thin she was, and she didn't want them thinking less of Kevin because of his comment about her weight.

Jenna called the meeting to order, then Heather read the minutes from last week's meeting. "Any corrections or additions?" she asked.

"Sounds fine to me," Manda said, sitting across the table.

"Me too," said Livvy.

"What new business do we have to discuss?" Jenna asked.

"I propose a craft project," Livvy said, her face growing a bit pink as soon as she spoke up.

"You mean like *making* something . . . with our *hands*?" Manda asked. She looked horrified.

"Sure." Livvy nodded. "To raise money for our club."

Jenna jumped on the idea. "We could use some extra

cash, you know, for costumes and things . . . when we put on ballet presentations for our families."

"I like the idea," Heather said. "But what'll we make?"

"My mom's a little over the edge about birdhouses," Manda said. "Maybe we could get some old wood somewhere and make some, then paint them real cute."

"Yeah, that's a possibility," Livvy agreed. But Heather could tell she wasn't overly wild about the idea. No one else seemed to be, either. "What about collecting recipes . . . healthy ones, for the athletically inclined?" suggested Livvy.

"Hey, great idea," Heather said.

Manda, too, was swayed by either their enthusiasm or the fact that she truly enjoyed creating healthy foods and drinks.

"So should we vote on doing a cookbook?" Jenna asked, with a flick of her dark brown hair.

The girls agreed. The vote was unanimous.

Jenna asked Livvy to coordinate the recipes, since the project had been her idea. "How much for our club cookbook?" asked Heather.

"Is five bucks too much?" asked Manda.

"I could run them off on my dad's computer printer," Livvy volunteered, "so it shouldn't cost us too much for production."

"Five dollars seems just right to me," Jenna said.

They voted. Five bucks it was. They also discussed sectioning off the book by recipes for specific times: After Training, Before Training, and High-Energy Snacks.

"This is a cool idea," Jenna said.

"Sure is," Heather said, wishing she'd thought of it.

Livvy smiled, quiet as usual. But Heather could see that her auburn-haired friend was very pleased.

"When do we start?" asked Manda.

"Tonight," Heather said. "That'll give me something to do while I'm waiting for my bum knee to mend."

The meeting was adjourned. Heather's mom emerged from the living room when they called to her. Serving up frozen vanilla yogurt with juicy red strawberries, Mom hummed as she worked.

"Thanks for letting us have our meeting here," Heather told her.

Mom glanced up, smiling. "Any time."

Manda whispered, "Let's tell your mom about our cookbook idea."

"Yeah, see what she says," Jenna said.

Heather filled her mother in on the fund-raising idea. "We'll take our finished product around to neighbors, family, and friends. So . . . what do you think?"

Mom was all for it. "I have a bunch of recipes to donate, if you'd like."

"Thanks!" Livvy said, bursting with delight.

The girls giggled at Livvy's enthusiasm. "Looks like *all* of us are on board with this," Jenna said.

Heather could see that it was true.

After the girls left, Heather helped her mom clean up the kitchen as best as she could with her hurt knee. "You have some terrific friends," Mom said as they wiped the table clean.

Heather thought how glad she was to have solid Christian girl friends. "And we're all on track for the Olympics. Isn't that the coolest thing?"

Mom nodded. "First, we've got to get your knee back to normal."

"Don't I know it." Heather sat down again, rubbing her kneecap. "I still can't believe Kevin and I fell like that."

Mom said no more, but busied herself with preparing supper. Heather hobbled upstairs to her room. She had intended to begin gathering a few recipes for the Girls Only cookbook, but weariness overtook her. She fell onto her bed, thinking she'd rest for a few minutes.

Soon, she was dreaming, flying in the air while Kevin sped on the ice. Heather felt so free, so limber . . . so high above the rink. But then Kevin dropped her flat on the ice, awakening her.

When she opened her eyes, she saw Joanne standing over her. "Uh . . . what's going on?" she asked, sitting up.

"Supper's ready, sleepyhead," came the little-girl reply.

"So soon?"

"Mom says you've been out for almost an hour."

An hour?

"Better come to the table," Joanne said, "so the food won't get cold."

She massaged her knee, feeling slightly dizzy as she moved toward the edge of the bed. "I'll be right down."

"Don't fall on the stairs," Joanne warned.

"Don't worry." Then she remembered something. "Oh, Joanne . . . have you been, uh, in my room?"

"Nope."

"Reading my devotional book, maybe?"

"Nope."

"You're sure?"

"I don't tell lies," Joanne insisted, wide-eyed.

"I didn't say you did," she replied, even though her sister had already dashed out of the room.

At supper, Dad prayed exceptionally long, blessing the food and asking the Lord "to bring strength and healing to my daughter's knee." There was some talk about the club recipe book, and Dad promised to purchase several copies. "I'll take them to the office and sell them there when they're finished."

"Really? You'd do that for the club?" Heather said, surprised her father was so interested.

Dad chuckled. "We have two secretaries who could use some trimming down. So sure. It'll help the cause."

Mom nodded. "Might just help someone feel healthier, too."

Kevin glared at Heather just then. His intense glower made her wonder. What was he trying to say? Surely not that he thought *she* needed to go on a diet!

CHAPTER 4

After supper, Heather got busy at the computer, going online to check through various sites featuring recipes. She decided the High-Energy Snacks section of the Girls Only cookbook might be her biggest interest.

Maybe if Kevin had eaten something like that, I wouldn't have fallen....

But she knew better. Anyone can fall on the ice. Energy or no energy. She'd have to forgive him, sooner or later.

Meanwhile, she printed off three different copyright-free on-line recipes: Bars of Iron with raisins, dark molasses, oats, and ginger; Powdered Milk Energy Bars; and Oat Bars with sesame seeds, dried apricots, and chopped almonds. Power food for sure. Livvy would be pleased.

By Monday, Heather's knee was much improved. Enough for her to skate freely around the rink. Coach McDonald was obviously pleased, but he didn't push for any lifts or jumps. And Kevin kept his mouth shut about further insults. *He better*, she thought.

After practice, when they'd arrived home, Heather noticed a mailer lying on the coffee table in the living room. "What's this?" she asked Kevin as he hung up his jacket.

"Looks like overnight mail." He came close and looked over her shoulder.

Mom had gone to the kitchen, so Heather called to her, asking if they could open the envelope. "Go ahead," Mom said. "It's probably the new pictures."

Heather felt her pulse quicken. Recently, Mom and Dad had hired a professional photographer from Denver. He'd met them several weeks ago, taking numerous rolls of film "to get a few good ones," the photographer had said.

"How do you think they turned out?" she asked her brother.

"Open it and see," Kevin said.

Tearing the envelope open, she discovered the proofs of her and Kevin. Dressed in ivory with dazzling Austrian sequins, they posed happily, taking bows. The shots had been taken at the finale of their two-minute original dance in Colorado Springs, at the World Arena. Every other weekend, they practiced there when they could get ice time.

One after another, Heather studied the pictures. "What do you think of them?" she asked Kevin.

"Cool," was all he said.

"But do you *like* them?"

"Yep. Don't you?"

She wasn't sure. Not exactly. In fact, the more she looked at them, scrutinizing every inch of each photo, the more she second-guessed the poses—the way the photographer had captured their "look."

"We don't look enough alike," she said softly.

Kevin squinted at the proofs. "I don't get it," he replied. "What's wrong?"

Their coach had trained them to move, breathe, and nearly think alike. On the ice, at least. When they skated in competition, or any event, for that matter, they always wore matching costumes, just like other ice-dancing partners. But these glitzy white costumes in the photos didn't offer the mirror image Heather had imagined. No, the long pants and double-breasted coat made Kevin look taller . . . *thinner*. Her outfit had been fashioned out of the same fabric, but the skirt, she decided as she inspected the picture, was too short. Showed too much of her leg.

She heard Kevin mutter something about being hungry. He headed off to the kitchen, probably to grab a quick snack before school started. Meanwhile, she took the pictures over to the bay window and sat in the overstuffed chair. Holding them up to the window, she stared at the poses. Slowly, she sifted through the pictures.

I hate these, she thought. But it wasn't the pictures she

despised. It was the reflection of herself in the camera that bugged her.

"Am I getting fat?" she asked Manda that afternoon on the phone.

Manda laughed. "You can't be serious."

"Come on, Manda," she insisted. If she wasn't serious, she wouldn't be asking her friend's opinion. "I'm not joking here. I want your honest opinion."

"Are you deaf? I *gave* you my honest opinion, girl. No way are you fat."

"Not even a little?"

Manda sighed into the phone. "Well, if you are, then it's invisible . . . or in your head."

"So, I'm a fathead?"

That got a laugh.

Heather continued. "Maybe you should take a look at these new pics that just arrived at my house."

"Of you?"

"Yeah, they're of Kevin and me." She propped the phone against her chin and shoulder as she slid the photos back into the large envelope. "Except my brother looks so tall and slender."

Like I used to, she thought.

"You're stick thin, Heather, and I'm not kidding."

She wished she could believe her friend. "Guess you'll

just have to see the pics," she said. "Then decide."

"Bring them to ballet in an hour. Jenna, Livvy, and I will give you our honest opinion ... that is, if we see the least hint of flab."

They said good-bye, and Heather hung up the phone.

At Natalie Johnston's ballet class, Heather worked extra hard during centerwork. And later, during pointe technique, she felt downright gloomy. Jenna and Livvy must've picked up on her mood, and during the break, when they stood around with small cartons of carrot juice and apple juice, Heather bought nothing to either drink or snack.

"Are you feeling all right?" asked Jenna.

"Uh-huh," she said.

"Want me to get you something?" Livvy offered.

"I'm fine, thanks."

"So what's with you today?" Jenna asked, grabbing a handful of carrot sticks.

"Nothing, why?"

"You just seem so ... uh, I don't know." Jenna crunched her carrots loudly.

"Out of it?" she said. "Not myself?"

Jenna eyed her without saying more.

Livvy came over and stood beside her. "Is training getting to you?"

She wondered if she should tell them what was bothering

her. But no, like Manda, they'd probably just laugh. Wouldn't understand that she'd begun to feel as fat as the pictures looked. As heavy as Kevin had said she was the day of their fall.

"Maybe you're tired," suggested Jenna. "Is that it?"

"I got some photos back from Denver," she began.

"Oh yeah, those," Jenna said. "Manda said you were bringing them to show us."

She wondered if Manda had also gone to the trouble of revealing what was troubling Heather. "Where's Manda, anyway?"

They turned to see their friend talking with Natalie near the piano. "Looks like she's tied up right now," said Livvy.

Heather cringed. She hoped Manda hadn't told Jenna and Livvy what she'd shared on the phone. For now, wanting to whittle down her figure was just *her* business.

It turned out the girls didn't stick around after ballet, as they often did. So Heather carried the envelope of photos home with her without ever showing them to her friends.

Just as well, she decided.

She didn't let on to her mother that she thought several of the photos made her look a little chunky. *Might just be the camera angle*, she thought. *Photos always make people look bigger*.

Mom seemed almost too excited about the portfolio

photos. She talked of nothing else at supper. Even took the pictures out and held them up as she stood at the foot of the table, opposite Dad. "Have you ever seen such great photos of *any* ice dancers?" she gushed to all of them. "Let alone *our* own children?"

Dad, too, seemed impressed, asking to see the pictures more closely. Mom and Dad, their heads together, made a big to-do about the shots. "We'll definitely use this photographer again, won't we, dear?" Dad said, his face bright with satisfaction.

Mom rested her hand on Dad's shoulder and beamed. "We couldn't be more proud of you both," she told Heather and Kevin.

Joanne and Tommy seemed interested, but only for a short time. After a while, they were more interested in knowing when and where dessert was than poring over photos of their older siblings.

"I'm gonna be as strong as Kevin when I grow up," Tommy said, squirming.

Joanne nodded her head, eyes twinkling. "And *I'm* going to look as slim as Kevin when I finish working out."

Nobody seemed to notice the remarks from the younger children. But Heather did, and she felt horrible. Crushed. Wasn't it obvious who Joanne and Tommy thought looked better? After all, Tommy had said Kevin was strong. And just now, Joanne minced no words about wanting to trim down, lose her baby fat—"look as slim as Kevin."

So . . . it was true what Kevin had said on the ice last Friday. She *was* too heavy.

Well, not for long. Starting this minute, she was going to make some changes. Some *big* changes!

CHAPTER 5

"Skinny is beautiful . . . skinny is beautiful," Heather chanted over and over.

She had been studying, doing her math homework in her room, when she got up to stretch. Going over to the window, she pulled back the curtains trimmed in pink rickrack and looked out.

It was mid-March, and the ground was beginning to peek through melting snow. No one could tell how much more snowfall they'd get this season. Snow was known to come in blizzard size this time of year in Alpine Lake, nestled high in the Rocky Mountains. But the fact that there were more than just a few brave blades of grass showing through the layer of white meant spring wasn't too far off.

With spring coming fast, the summer skate competition was on their heels. That's how Heather had been programmed to think. Skaters—any athletes involved in competitive sports—knew there was no time like the present to get it together. Never any time to waste.

Turning away from the window, she moved toward the tall, oval mirror and stared. She scanned every inch of herself. Then, glancing up at the poster of world-famous ice dancers Jayne Torvill and Christopher Dean, she looked at their overall body types.

They're stick thin. Just like the models in the magazine at Dottie Forster's Boutique, she thought.

Going back to her desk, she wondered how long before she might begin to notice a difference in her own weight. Then a brain wave hit. She hurried out of the room, heading to the bathroom. There she weighed herself—one hundred and five pounds. She hadn't lost a speck of fat since refusing dessert last evening! She'd also made a point of not eating or drinking during their break at ballet.

Mom had frowned, but only slightly, when Heather asked for cold cereal this morning instead of eggs. She'd only picked at her toast, not buttering it at all. And turned up her nose at warm cocoa.

Must take several days, she thought, determining to cut back on her food intake.

She'd do it, little by little, so no one would notice or protest. Maybe then Kevin would say nicer things about her, his long-time skating partner. And maybe Joanne would say she wanted to be as slim and pretty as her big *sister* when she grew up.

She knew Mom would be her biggest hurdle. Her mother was hooked into healthy foods, wanted her kids to feel good—"the picture of health," Mom often said.

Well, Heather had gone Mom's route for nearly twelve years. It was time to do things *her* way.

When she finished her math assignment, she stayed at her desk. For a while, she doodled on a blank sheet of paper, daydreaming as she did. Then she began to write her name in cursive, over and over: *Heather Elayne Bock . . .*

Thinking back to the photos—the ones she hadn't shown to her Girls Only Club members—Heather imagined what it would be like to ice-dance with someone other than Kevin. Brother-sister pairs were supposed to be ideal. At least, until a skater reached the late teens. But even then, Coach Mc-Donald had always said a brother-sister team was the way to go. The best hope for Junior Olympics.

Her biggest hang-up was having to look so much like Kevin. She was her own person, wasn't she? Yet they dressed nearly exactly alike on the ice, moving in perfect symmetry, smiling on cue, flowing to the music, performing difficult stunts.

Like puppets on a string, she thought. *Look-alike puppets*.

It had been Mom's idea to get them started in ice dancing. They worked so well together, maybe because they were less than two years apart in age. And they both shared a love for skating, as well as being part of a close-knit homeschooling family.

Their hair color was identical. They even had the same shade of blue eyes. Twins in every way except age. That is, if you could call yourself a twin with your *older* brother. Kevin was thirteen, going on fourteen, and as skinny as a handrail. She, on the other hand, was a girl, not even a teen. A "heavy" girl, at that.

Lifting up her sweater cautiously, Heather looked at herself in the mirror, trying to see her ribs. Someday soon, she'd be able to count them. That was her goal—to get down to nothing. Just like the magazine models. She'd show her skating partner. Little sister, too.

As for Mom, Heather felt pent-up anger toward her. She didn't quite know why. Unless it had something to do with being pushed too hard and fast into a mold. The brother-sister thing? Maybe that was the trigger.

Whatever it was, Heather was unhappy. Dissatisfied with how she looked.

"What're you doing?" Joanne asked, standing at the door, looking in.

Startled, Heather pushed down her sweater quickly. "Don't you ever knock?"

Joanne smirked and opened the door wider, coming into

the room. "I saw you peeking under your sweater," she said in an accusing tone. "That's really weird, you know."

"Mind your own business."

"What were you looking at?" came the next awkward question.

"Listen, Joanne, I'm really tired, and it's late. Don't you have to brush your teeth or something?"

"Only when you tell me what you were doing in the mirror." Her sister marched over to the dresser and leaned on the front, her hands on her hips.

"Who said you could even come in here?"

"*You* didn't stop me." Joanne's eyes were serious.

"Well, I'm asking you to leave. Now."

Her sister's eyes were blinking fast. "Don't be so mean, Heather. That's not what Jesus wants you to be."

"I'm *not* being anything to you. Now, get out of my room!" With that, she scooted Joanne along toward the door.

"I'm telling Mommy."

"Please do."

Joanne turned and stuck out her tongue. "Don't make me!"

"Well, if *you* don't tell Mom, then I will."

That silenced Joanne. She pulled another face and ran off down the hall to her own room.

Relieved, Heather turned her attention back to the mirror. This time, she kept her sweater down. Instead, she leaned over and rolled up her jeans. She looked long and hard at her ankles. "Could use some slimming," she whispered.

Though she was preoccupied with her figure, Heather thought through the steps and moves to the American Waltz as she showered. Letting the water beat on her back, she performed the dance in her head. She and Kevin planned to skate for the Novice level silver dance test next November. Their first shot at Novice. They would present the dance in July at the summer event, too. It was a good chance to practice and compete with a "live" audience.

The meter was in three-four time: *one*, two, three—with the accent on the first beat, a typical waltz beat. The tempo was sixty-six measures of three beats. One-hundred-ninety-eight beats per minute. Smooth and flowing, the waltz had stylish direction changes, graceful and uniform in pace. Knees bent, corresponding with the heavy beat in each measure, they would skate in perfect unison.

Ice dancing was much different from pairs skating. In pairs, there were side-by-side jumps, spins, and other moves. But ice dancing was all about footwork—mostly fancy steps performed in precise time with dance rhythms such as the polka, tango, waltz, and fox-trot. The steps of each dance were drawn on a diagram of the ice rink. The International Skating Union and U.S. Figure Skating Association preserved music libraries with suitable music for each of the compulsory dances. Techniques such as conformity to the style and mood of the music, placement of steps, movements of both partners, good form and style, edge technique, dancing to the beat, and character of the music were essential elements for a top mark by a judge.

As much as Heather wanted to test to the next level, which would set them up for the Junior level international competition, possibly as soon as next year, she struggled with the *twin image* thing. How far did they have to take it? Would she ever be her own person?

On the other hand, she knew better than to question her future. Ice dancing with Kevin was the surest way to Olympic fame and success. She'd gone through tough times, struggling with the notion of becoming a free skater, going it alone. In the end, though, she knew where she belonged— as Kevin's skating partner. They were fantastic skaters together. Coach McDonald told them so, and often. They were headed for gold.

Someday.

CHAPTER 6

At breakfast, Heather sat down to a full plate of food. Mom had been up very early, making her delicious whole-grain bread and homemade granola cereal. There was fresh fruit, too—cantaloupe, bananas, and strawberries.

Heather looked down at the plate, just staring at it. Mom had gone out of her way to prepare a good "skater's breakfast," as she liked to call it. Small dishes of yogurt were set off to the left of both hers and Kevin's plates.

I'm not hungry, Heather told herself.

Knowing full well that Mom would expect her to eat heartily, she slowly ate two spoonfuls of granola softened with skim milk. She figured if she took her time, ate at a snail's pace, she could prolong the meal until it was too late to finish.

"You're not eating, Heather." Mom had noticed.

She shrugged. "Don't feel like it."

Mom glanced at the wall clock. "Well, you can't sit there and just look at your food. Not when you're expected to train at the rink this morning. You'll need the nourishment."

"I'm not hungry."

Kevin looked up. "Since when?"

"Since now." With that, she got up from the table and trounced out of the kitchen. She could hear the not-so-discreet comments whispered in her absence. This was just the beginning, and Mom did *not* understand.

She was actually a little surprised that she got through the day till lunch without feeling too weak or light-headed. No symptoms she might've experienced by now, due to her new eat-less approach to life, seemed to be evident. Best of all, she'd felt lighter while on the ice, after scarcely any breakfast. A great feeling.

After their homeschool sessions, she decided to head over to Natalie's ballet studio, a short walk away. Every other Wednesday, Natalie offered "free workout" sessions for super-dedicated students. Heather wanted to work on limbering up her knee a little while.

In the locker room, she dressed in her warm-up tights, then sneaked a peek at herself in the full-length mirror.

Still too fat, she thought, noticing the slightest pad of flesh around her knees.

Livvy Hudson soon caught up with her at the practice barre. "You look tired," she said. "Feeling okay?"

Heather nodded. Now wasn't the time to get into the "going skeletal" thing with Livvy. Her friend would never understand. Besides, Livvy was an only child. How could she begin to relate to a younger sister's flippant remark? Or an older brother's crude comment? All good motivations to drop some pounds.

Livvy was pushing harder, doing longer stretches than Heather had the energy for. "Are you sure you're all right?" Livvy asked.

"Why shouldn't I be?" This was annoying, coming from Alpine Lake's award-winning free skater.

Livvy eyed her curiously. "I don't know. It's just that—"

"What?"

"You look pale, that's all."

Heather smirked and increased her efforts, still cautious of her knee. She refused to accept the fact that she *did* feel a bit weak. After more stretches and moves, she drank lots of water. *Water never made anyone fat*, Heather thought. The water seemed to take the edge off her hunger pangs.

During break, she purposely denied herself her usual snack intake, pitching half the turkey and Swiss cheese sandwich her mother had packed—*"just in case you're hungry,"* Mom had said.

Jenna caught her trashing part of the food. "Whoa, girl, isn't that the whole-grain, super-good stuff your mom bakes?"

"Yeah, so?"

Jenna's eyes were intent on her, squinting nearly shut as they walked to the small room just off the studio area. Natalie's students hung out there before continuing workout sessions.

Manda was waiting, obviously glad to see them. Jen chatted with Manda for a moment, then fell into a plump chair, turning to Heather. "Hey, that's great stuff." She meant the sandwich. "Next time you don't want your mom's good snacks, just hand them over. Okay?"

Manda got a kick out of Jen's comment. "Sounds like she's very serious," Manda said, munching on a celery stick.

Jenna smiled. "I wish *my* mother had time to bake bread."

Livvy joined them about the time Heather was finished. "Are you leaving so soon?"

"Yep," Heather said. "Gotta run."

"Where to?" asked Jenna.

"Yeah, what's the rush?" asked Manda.

The room was filling up with other ballet students. "I need some fresh air," she said, waving at the girls. She purposely kept moving, otherwise one of them might call her back. Might try to get to the bottom of what was going on in her head. She had to avoid more conversation at all costs.

Heather headed straight to the mall ice rink, taking time

to warm up again before ever going out on the ice. Her knee still required special attention after the fall last Friday. So she spent extra time—more than usual—stretching her quad muscles. They were the muscles that began just below the outside of her hips, ending just below her knee.

She stood erect and tilted her hips backward just a bit. Then, lifting her right knee so her right thigh was parallel to the floor, she grabbed her ankle with her right hand. She went through the exercise process, repeating the *quadriceps* stretch several times on both sides. Careful not to bounce or stretch at all in short surges—because bouncing can tear muscles—she used constant pressure during the fifteen-second segments. Then she rested, only to repeat the stretch.

On the ice now, she stroked forward on the inside edge of her right skate, several times around the rink. Other skaters were practicing, too. Some of them were Natalie Johnston's beginning skaters. Natalie was not only the best ballet teacher around, she also taught a few skating classes in Alpine Lake.

Since bruising her knee, Heather knew she needed time on the ice, limbering up again. She wanted to get back her confidence. Kevin's words—*"If you weren't so heavy"*—still rang loudly in her ears.

"Hey, looking good!" one of Natalie's students called to her.

She waved to the boy across the ice. It was Micky Waller, Natalie's best male free skater. How long had it been since a cute boy had said something like that to her? On the ice, no less?

So . . . her idea to cool it with eating was paying off. In fact, Micky was actually still smiling at her from across the rink. Really grinning now as he turned and skated toward her.

Nice run of blade, she thought as he powerfully stroked, looking like a top-level skater—well balanced and flowing well over the ice. She wondered how long Micky had been training with Natalie.

"Haven't seen you for a while," he said, falling into rhythm with her.

"I'm here nearly every day," she said. "How about you?"

"Me too."

She wondered what Kevin would think when he showed up. Mom and Dad weren't exactly thrilled about her hanging out with boys. Her parents were pretty strict about the boy-girl thing. She figured she wouldn't be dating till she was twenty-five or older. At least, that's how Dad joked about it.

Micky was close to Kevin's age, she was pretty sure. And she wasn't so much interested in him as a friend as she was curious. He'd singled her out from all the other girls on the ice just now.

Skinny is beautiful, she thought, determined to lose even more of her excess weight in the coming days and weeks.

Obviously, Micky had noticed. How long before Kevin and Joanne did, too?

At the rate she was going, she could drop to a size zero in the blink of an eye. And she would. Nothing could stop her now.

CHAPTER 7

She should've known.

Heather got into it with Mom the second she pushed back from the table after only a few bites of sirloin steak, rich gravy, and baked potatoes.

"Honey, what's wrong?" Mom's frown lines grew deeper by the second.

"I'm full." She hoped her excuse would fly. If not, she had no idea what she'd say or do next.

Dad looked puzzled from his end of the table. Now *he* was getting in on the question thing. "Heather, are you ill?"

"Just full, Daddy."

"It's not like you," Mom insisted.

Joanne stared across the table, her little eyes peering at Heather. She was only slightly taller than the table. Usually, they had her sit on the telephone book or other stacked books. Tonight, though, Joanne looked like a midget. "If Heather worked out enough, she'd be hungrier," came her little voice.

Tommy began nodding his head, joining in the campaign.

"What do *you* know about working out?" Heather shot back.

"Mommy!" whined Joanne.

"That's quite enough, young lady," Mom directed her rebuke to Heather.

"What did *I* say?" Heather was fed up. She wanted to leave the table, but she tried not to lose it in front of Dad. Her father liked a peaceful atmosphere at mealtime.

Mom's expression turned from a frown to a pretend scowl. She stood there, scrutinizing Heather. "Who *are* you, really, and what did you do with my daughter?" Mom quipped.

Tommy looked completely confused, then started to laugh.

"Yeah, what did you do with my big sister, Heather, who used to like to eat?" Joanne asked, giggling a little till Dad intervened.

"Let's get back to the business of supper," Dad said firmly, yet softly. "Your mother made a terrific meal." He looked over at Mom, winking at her. "Thanks, dear."

Mom merely nodded, still looking a bit frazzled. "Save room for some delicious no-fat frozen yogurt for dessert," was all she said.

Yogurt, either low-fat or no-fat, did not sound very appealing to Heather. She wished she could excuse herself and get a head start on Mom's hefty history assignment before the prayer service tonight at church. But she thought better of it, staying put. The last thing she wanted to do, judging from her parents' serious expressions, was cause another ruckus.

Heather was more than miserable during the Bible study and prayer meeting. Kevin took Joanne and Tommy off to the children's classes. Her older brother had been assisting the junior boys' group recently.

Their youth pastor was out of town, so the teens and preteens were stuck in the main service with the adults. Several other kids were sitting with their parents, slumped down in the pew like it was some horribly hideous thing.

She was smarter than that. Besides, Dad had shown his disapproval after supper. He'd made it obvious to her by hanging around the kitchen while she and Mom and Joanne cleaned things up. It was like he didn't trust her or something. Maybe he thought she was going to continue the scuffle with Mom in the privacy of the kitchen.

Well, she had no intention of keeping the conflict going. Mom was behaving like a good mother, encouraging Heather to eat and enjoy her great cooking. How could that be Mom's fault?

So here they were, all lined up in the church pew. Dad, Mom, and her. Of all the nights for youth group to be canceled. She'd have to grin and bear it, because she wouldn't risk catching Dad's eye during the Bible study or prayer. She knew better. She also knew how to conduct herself in church, whether Wednesday night or Sunday morning. She'd been raised in this church, attending nearly every time the doors were open.

Yet this evening, she felt she was only partially present. Sure, she was sitting there, hearing the minister expound on one of the epistles, the apostle's letter to a church in Corinth. But her heart and brain were elsewhere. She could hardly wait to drop by Dottie Forster's Boutique tomorrow. Maybe she'd ask Dottie if she needed the teen magazine, the one with the skinny models. If not, maybe Dottie would let her borrow it. She really hoped so. She wanted to compare her ankles and other parts of her body with the very thin girls in the fashion section.

" 'Godliness has value for all things . . .' " Their pastor's words, a direct quote from the Bible, took her off guard. She'd read precisely the same thing in her own devotional book a few days ago. What was going on?

After church, there was a message on their voice mail. She could hear Livvy's voice, but it sounded strange . . . far away. "Is something wrong?" she asked Mom.

"Not that I know of." Mom came over and listened to Livvy's message. "I see what you mean, though. Does sound a bit garbled."

For a second, Heather wondered if Livvy was sick. But when she called her, Heather discovered a bubbly friend waiting by the phone. "You'll never guess what," Livvy said.

"What's going on? You sound breathless."

Livvy laughed softly. "This is really amazing."

"What is?"

"Micky Waller—remember him?—wants to give you a call."

Heather sucked in her breath. "What?"

"Yeah, I ran into him at the mall rink late this afternoon," Livvy said. "He asked me for your number."

She groaned inwardly. "Uh, you didn't just give it to him, I hope."

"That's why I'm calling *you*, silly," Livvy replied. "So . . . what should I do?"

She had to think about that. "Better not . . . at least for now."

"How come?"

Glancing toward the living room, she spied Dad sitting in his easy chair, reading a magazine. "I just better not," she said more softly.

"I don't get it. Micky just wants to talk to you."

"I know, but it's a mistake. Bad timing."

"Know what *I* think?" Livvy wasn't giving up.

Heather fell silent, not too eager to hear what was on her

friend's mind. But she listened.

"Heather, you still there?"

"Go ahead. I'm listening . . ."

"I think Micky's really cute," Livvy said. "You'd be crazy not to let him call you."

Heather sighed. "Maybe what he really wants is *your* phone number."

"I don't know. To tell you the truth, my dad's dragging his feet about me starting to talk to boys on the phone. And Grandma Hudson would probably hit the roof."

"Yeah."

"Maybe it's for the best," Livvy volunteered. "Liking boys can get very distracting."

"Right. We both have too much work to do . . . to reach our skating goals. There's really no time for boys." She'd said what she really believed.

Just maybe Dad was—right now—overhearing her end of the conversation. What she'd said about boys might earn her some points. After all, she needed to do what she could to make up for behaving badly at supper.

After she hung up, she tried to slip upstairs to her room without being noticed. But Dad called to her just as she reached the hallway. "Heather, do you have a minute?"

"Sure, Daddy." She bounded into the living room, sitting across from him on the sofa.

He put his magazine away, sliding it under the coffee table. "I'm glad we have this chance to chat," he began. "Your mother and I are concerned. You ate very little today—far less than usual. Is something upsetting you?"

She wouldn't unload on him, spill out the remarks that had gotten her thinking about her weight in the first place. Dad wouldn't be interested in either Joanne's or Kevin's comments, either. "I'm fine," she said.

He leaned back in his chair. "You can say you're fine, but I think there may be something behind all this."

"Like what?"

Dad was smiling. "I was hoping you could tell *me*."

Just then, Mom came into the room. She was carrying the stack of professional photo proofs. Sitting down, she suddenly looked very tired as she shuffled through them. "I hope your not eating doesn't have anything to do with these wonderful pictures of you and Kevin," Mom said softly.

What could Heather say?

She noticed the dark circles under her dad's normally bright blue eyes. Tonight, his hair was a bit disheveled. Maybe from raking his long fingers through it while Heather was talking nonsense on the phone with Livvy. Yep, that's probably what was bothering him.

"I don't want either of you to worry," she said, getting up. "I'm feeling just great."

"But you're pale," Mom said, reaching out her hand.

"I feel fine." She didn't really feel all that terrific, but there was no turning back now. She was on track to reach her goal—do or die.

CHAPTER 8

Dottie Forster's eyes actually lit up when Heather strolled nonchalantly into the beauty salon after homeschool hours. "What can I do for you, cutie?" asked the middle-aged beautician.

"Just thought I'd check in." Heather eyed the magazine rack, hoping Dottie wouldn't notice. "Everything cool here?"

"Always." Dottie turned the gray-haired woman who was getting a color. The client faced away from the mirror. "Need a trim?" asked Dottie.

"Sometime, just not today."

"Okay. Call me whenever."

Heather sat down, picking up the first magazine she saw. "Mind if I sit here?"

"No problem, and help yourself to some magazines," Dottie said. "I get so many piled up here . . . lots of them are out-of-date, too. Take them, if you like."

Mom had always said that Dottie had been around the block more than once. Was this evidence of her perception? Could Dottie tell by the look in Heather's eyes that she was on the lookout for that one special teen magazine?

Wow, and I thought Mom was bad....

She sat there reading one monotonous magazine after another. At last, she finally found the courage to pick up the one she *really* wanted. She looked at the date. Too bad, it was the March issue, the current month. Dottie wouldn't be ready to let this one go. But Heather asked anyway.

"Hmm, let's see," Dottie said, coming over. She thumbed through the magazine, never hesitating on the article that had caught Heather's attention. "Sure, take it. I have plenty of teen mags floating around here."

Heather was overjoyed. "Are you sure?"

Dottie waved her hands. "I'm sure ... I'm sure. Hey, enjoy."

All the way home, she stared at the lanky models—six pages worth. The girls were all very tall. Lots taller than she was. But then, she knew she still had several years left to grow. Being tall was a major plus in the fashion circles. But being not only petite but short gave a skater somewhat of an advantage. "You're closer to the ice," Livvy's grandmother liked to say.

Kevin had often told Heather that, too. "The closer you are to the ice, the softer the fall."

Her response was to laugh it off. Now she wasn't sure. Height gave a girl the lean lines Heather longed for. Both Dad and Mom were fairly tall. And Kevin was starting to shoot up, too. So there was hope for her.

Nearing her house, she rolled up the magazine and stuffed it into her backpack. No need to share this with Mom. She'd freak for sure, figure that Heather had gotten the notion not to eat merely from these skinny models. Well, maybe that had started the ball rolling, but there was much more to it. More than Heather cared to discuss with her mother. Or anyone.

Finishing off her homework, Heather rushed to the basement. Her parents had set up a workout area there for her and Kevin especially. Dad used it often, though. Mom too. And sometimes she saw Joanne there trying to lift the smallest weights.

"Physical training is of some value," the Bible verse stated.

She decided to set the treadmill for forty-five minutes this time, upping the amount of time by fifteen minutes. Each day, she planned to increase her time. No longer was she satisfied with her performance. She felt compelled to push harder, go farther, work longer.

I can get as thin as those models, she thought. *I can!*

She visualized herself as one of the girls in the magazine. Sporting the sleek, thin jeans and tight boots. Yeah, she could fit into a size nothing real soon.

When Mom called, Heather scarcely heard. Joanne came running downstairs to alert her. "Mom's been calling. Didn't you hear?"

"Huh?"

"Mom wants you to make the salad. Hurry!" The younger girl turned and left the room.

Heather had spaced out on the time completely. Gone past her set time on the treadmill. She was actually beginning to love this workout regimen. Besides that, Coach McDonald would be pleased when he realized how terrific her stamina was.

Tomorrow she would check herself on the ice. Surely, the additional exercising would benefit her skating. Not to mention getting her slimmed way down.

She went to make the vegetable salad for Mom. Then, when she was finished, she climbed the steps to the second floor. She was surprised to see Joanne coming out of *her* private domain—Heather's bedroom. Actually, it seemed that she'd caught her little sister in the act of something. Just what, she didn't know. "What're you doing in my room?" she demanded.

"Oh, nothing." Joanne shrugged her shoulders innocently enough.

"Right . . . nothing. You keep saying that." Heather took

the last three steps with a single bound. She towered over her little sister. "I know you were in my room."

"I just borrowed something, that's all."

"Borrowed what?"

Joanne shrugged again, tilting her mischievous little head to the side.

"C'mon," Heather urged.

But Joanne shook her head silently.

"So you're not going to tell me? Is that it?" She was mad. "I won't play twenty questions with you. You'd better tell me now or . . ."

How far should she take this? If Mom was witness to this exchange, they'd both be in trouble. They'd been taught to respect not only each other's privacy, but to treat each other with esteem. "Where's Mom?" she asked, curious.

Joanne shook her head. "I don't know."

"I think you do," she shot back. "And you know you're not supposed to snoop in my room or anyone else's. So . . . Mom must be downstairs somewhere."

Tommy emerged from his own bedroom, a Lego creation in his hand. "Mommy's in the family room."

Heather straightened. "Do you really have to eavesdrop?"

"What's *that* mean?" Poor Tommy. He was stuck in the middle.

She glared at both of them. "Look, you two . . ." She stopped from almost lashing out at her brother and sister. It was a good thing she'd bit her tongue, because Mom's footsteps were on the stairs just now.

Heather turned to see her mother's arms loaded down with folded laundry. "I could use some help, kids," Mom said. Usually, she didn't have to say much about helping. They all liked to pitch in and pull their weight with chores.

Joanne and Tommy stood at the landing, waiting with arms outstretched.

Perfect little brother and sister, she thought, staring at the twosome. But she knew the truth. They weren't even close to perfect.

Sooner or later, Mom would find it out.

When the laundry was put away, Heather closed the door to her room. Looking around, she tried to figure out what Joanne had borrowed. She went to her dresser. No drawers were hanging out. Nothing seemed to be missing. At least, not that she noticed. Her bed wasn't even rumpled. So what did Joanne need so badly that she was willing to risk getting caught?

Going to her mirror, Heather stared at her reflection. *Cool outfit*, she thought, looking at the gold and black jogging suit. Mom had purchased it during the after-Christmas sales a couple of months back. She especially liked the color gold, which seemed to point out the blond highlights in her hair.

Turning her back to the mirror, she glimpsed the back of her. She thought she *might* be a teeny bit thinner. But she couldn't be sure. Not without undressing. Tonight, after her shower, she would check to see how she *really* looked.

Just then, a knock came at her door. She hurried to see who was there.

It was Mom, standing in the hallway. "Heather, I'd like to talk with you when you have a minute."

The tone of Mom's voice spelled trouble. What had Joanne told her? Or was Tommy the culprit this time?

"Am I in trouble?" she said before thinking. She'd practically told on herself.

"Sounds like you have a guilty conscience." Mom smiled, reaching out to squeeze her arm. "Meet me in my bedroom in a few minutes. Okay, honey?"

Now she *knew* this was serious. "Sure, Mom."

She slipped her jogger top over her head, wearing only the short-sleeved black T-shirt underneath. One more quick look in the mirror gave her the nerve to think about what little she could get by with eating at supper. She'd smelled the meaty aroma of roasted chicken. One of Mom's most delicious recipes. Delicious or not, Heather had a plan that did not include eating much of the specialty dish at all. Sure, her stomach had been rumbling all day long. She'd fought hard against the ongoing hunger pangs. Pretty soon they'd go away. They *had* to.

Mom was waiting for her in the master suite, standing by the window. "What's up?" Heather asked, hoping for an off-the-cuff reply. But Mom motioned for her to close the door. Another danger sign.

They stood at the foot of her parents' bed for a moment. Then Mom suggested they sit down. So Heather chose to perch on the bed, while her mother sat in a chair across the room. "I wish I didn't have to talk to you about this," Mom began. "I think by now you should know better."

Here it comes ...

"I happened to overhear your conversation with Joanne earlier." Mom paused, probably searching for the right words. "Your sister looks up to you, Heather. She's learning from you each day. Tommy too."

Heather wished Mom would bring Kevin into this lecture. Why wasn't her older brother included? Was *he* the ideal role model?

She refused to mention Kevin. She kept quiet—something she should've done when she first caught Joanne scurrying out of her room. Just what did Mom know about any of *that*?

"We've studied very thoroughly godly character traits," Mom continued.

True. Heather—the whole family, for that matter—had studied and learned thoroughly the Bible-based attributes. She could recite them, each one corresponding to a fruit of the Spirit. But then, so could Joanne and Tommy.

Why was Mom picking on *her*?

"I'd like you to go easy on your sister ... about whatever she was borrowing," Mom said straight out.

"But Joanne's constantly messing around in my room."

"Be gentle and patient with her when you bring it up

again. All right?" Mom's eyes reflected her own kind spirit.

Yet Heather could not contain her anger about the situation. "I'm sick and tired of Joanne waltzing in and out of my room at will. She's doing something in there. I know she is!"

"I'll talk to Joanne," Mom said quickly. "In the meantime, can you please watch your attitude a bit?"

Watch my attitude? She felt the anger rising. But she wouldn't sass her mother. The ultimate no-no.

She ought to be sorry for her tone of voice with Joanne. She ought to act as an example to her younger sister. But she didn't feel a bit sorry. Not at the moment.

Maybe not at all.

CHAPTER 9

Any other evening, Heather might've asked to be excused and hurried off to bed. Homework was completed and double-checked, just the way Mom liked it. But Dad was probably waiting in the living room eager to get family devotions going. There was no getting out of that. And she didn't really want to dodge out of it. Just needed some space.

Her head ached and her stomach growled. She knew she should've eaten more of Mom's tasty and tender chicken. She'd hardly eaten a speck of food.

My own fault, she thought, sitting next to her little brother.

Quietly, she turned to the Bible. Dad had asked specifically for Galatians 5:14. She should've recognized the verse before she ever turned to it. Dad had helped both her and Kevin memorize the passage years ago. Even before little

Joanne and Tommy had come into their lives through adoption.

The living room was quiet. Dad and Mom sat together on the sofa. Joanne was perched at Dad's feet. Heather and Tommy were snug on the loveseat.

Dad started with a general, family-type prayer. Then he asked her to begin reading.

" 'The entire law is summed up in a single command: Love your neighbor as yourself,' " she read, feeling her face growing warm. But the room remained still.

Heather fully expected Dad to comment on the verse, the way he usually did. But not tonight. Instead, Dad asked Kevin to read another Scripture, which just so happened to be about getting along with others in the family of God.

So was this a specific lesson for the whole family? Or was Dad focusing in on her?

No use getting huffy about it. Better to listen and learn—and repent, as Dad always suggested—than to get herself in a stew over something minor. She and Joanne didn't need to be at each other's throats.

Still, the idea of Joanne getting by with snooping bugged her. She was starting to feel she had no control over much of anything anymore.

While Dad talked about the importance of getting along in a cheerful manner, Heather let her mind wander. She thought about the things she *could* control in her life. Things like her food intake. Things like how many hours a day she exercised. And nope, she wasn't ready to give up trying to lose weight. No matter what anybody said.

By the time Dad was finished talking and reading from his Bible, she was eager to get to bed. Morning couldn't come early enough for her this night. She could hardly wait to hit the ice. Besides that, tomorrow afternoon was the next Girls Only Club meeting. She had several fantastic recipes to add to Livvy's cookbook.

To think she was collecting recipes when she'd given up eating. What a hoot!

Before turning out the light, Heather curled up on her bed. She skimmed through the teen magazine once again, enjoying the pictures immensely. She wondered how thin she'd look this time next week. Would anyone notice? What would Coach say? How about Kevin?

Kevin . . .

At least, maybe he wouldn't drop her on their lifts. Soon, she'd be lots lighter. That alone was good enough reason to shed some pounds.

Scooting off the bed, she went and stood in front of the large floor mirror in the corner of the room. Yes, she could see the slightest changes—or she thought so. Wearing only her baby-doll pajamas, she thought her legs . . . and maybe her ankles, too, seemed a little slimmer. Yes, they *were* thinner. She was sure of it.

Good, she thought. *I'm on the right track*.

But when she finally did slip into bed, she had a hard time relaxing. Falling asleep had never been a problem before. The gnawing in her stomach and the dizzy feeling in her head kept her tossing and turning.

Around eleven, she got up and tiptoed downstairs. One little bite of a graham cracker and a swallow of milk wouldn't hurt anything. She had to do something. So she crept out of her room and down the stairs.

She was surprised to find Mom downstairs, too. Sitting in the dark, her mother was praying in the living room. Heather wouldn't have known she was there, except she heard someone whispering her name as she came down the steps.

"Lord, please help my Heather . . . whatever is bothering her," Mom prayed softly.

Heather swallowed hard. She didn't know what to think. Mom, up this late? How would she feel when five o'clock in the morning rolled around?

It wasn't hard for Heather to know how *she* would feel, dragging out of bed. Ten hours of sleep a night was essential for active athletes during the growing years. Physical exertion demanded recovery time. She'd pushed her body extra hard today, working out on the treadmill far longer than ever. She knew from past experience she could only stretch her limits so far.

She would pay dearly if she didn't get proper rest. And Coach McDonald would see right through the balance and concentration problems that were sure to crop up. Even after only one night of poor sleep.

Hurrying to the kitchen, she ate three crackers, then poured a tiny bit of milk. She limited herself to just one third of a cup. Tomorrow, she'd do better about not snacking. She promised herself.

 CHAPTER 10

At breakfast, Heather purposely suppressed the urge to eat. She also made excuses about why she was late coming to the table. "I couldn't find the warm-up suit I wanted," she said, feeling terribly tired and irritable.

Mom's eyebrows rose briefly, but she said nothing. Dad was nowhere around, as he'd gotten an even earlier start on his day. He wasn't there to either witness her explanation or intervene.

Kevin, though, stared at her curiously. "What's with the zero appetite?" he asked.

Before Heather could say a word, their mother quickly changed the subject. So nothing more was said, and Heather was relieved. She was too exhausted to put up much of a fight. Especially with Kevin.

After sitting only a few minutes at the table, she pushed

back her half-full glass of orange juice. She'd taken only a few bites of her fresh pear, then bravely she asked to be excused.

Thankfully, Mom seemed cool enough about it. *Good*, thought Heather. She could put her plan into action more easily with some breathing room.

"Someone should call the phone company about our voice mail," Kevin reminded Mom.

"Yeah, it's messed up," Heather spoke up, remembering Livvy's hazy message.

"I'll look into it," Mom assured them. She also told them about getting together with two other homeschooling families. "We plan to meet here after lunch."

Kevin seemed interested. "We're starting another new history unit, right?"

Mom nodded. "It's time we delve more deeply into the American Constitution."

"Cool," Heather said.

At least it wasn't another one of Mom's nutrition units. The history study with other families of kids was great news. Joanne and Tommy would be studying on different levels, and Heather and Kevin would pair up with some of the older kids. Mom was good about having all four of them work on similar themes, but she also had a knack for bringing the subject matter down to each of their comprehension levels, even including Joanne with mazes, puzzles, and age-appropriate material.

Somehow, Heather made it through her morning ice session. But she was really beginning to drag as she sat on the bench to remove her skates. Kevin waited around for her, leaning on the barrier. He was obviously impatient, too, by the way he shuffled about. But he didn't bring up anything troublesome, and she was glad.

The walk home seemed longer than usual. Heather's legs felt more like rubber than flesh and bone and muscle. Mom hadn't accompanied them to the early-morning session. Often, she let them walk to and from. Today, though, Heather wished her mother had driven them.

"What's wrong with you?" Kevin asked.

"Nothing."

"Anyone can see you're worn out," he persisted.

She sighed. Her brother didn't need to know that she'd been up prowling around the kitchen for something to eat so late in the night. "I'm fine," she insisted.

"Say what you like. I can see you're exhausted."

"Why don't you just . . . leave me alone?"

"Oh yeah, sure . . . that's a great suggestion." He paused as they walked in silence. Then—"So is it really none of my business that my skating partner is falling off balance and skating way under her ability today?"

He had her. She scuffed her feet against the sidewalk, saying nothing.

"Look, Heather, if you have to go on some stupid crash

course, or whatever it is you're doing to your body, I think you'd better bounce it off me first. Okay?"

"Says who?"

"Coach, for one . . . and Mom and Dad, too, since they're paying big bucks for our training. In case you forgot. They're behind us all the way, helping us push ourselves ahead to our goal." He stopped and turned to look at her. "It *is* still your goal, right?"

"To get to Junior Olympics, sure." There was no question in her mind.

"Then, how about if you start eating?"

They began walking again. This time, she forged ahead, leaving her brother behind.

"Aw, don't do this," Kevin called to her.

"Don't do *what*—walk faster than you?" She didn't even stop to glance over her shoulder. She was losing it faster than her own stride.

"Your head's jumbled," he said flatly.

That got her attention. She turned and waited for him. "Since when is it fair for you to call all the shots for us?"

"It's fair only when I see my sister doing harm to herself." He sighed loudly. "I wish I knew what was bugging you."

"Whatever." She turned away.

"No, Heather, I mean it." Kevin reached and grabbed her arm. "You're not heavy, if that's what you think." His eyes were kind. He *was* concerned.

"We're not having this conversation." And that was the end of it.

Weary before the day had scarcely begun, she mustered up enough energy to run ahead of him. At her side, her skates flip-flopped nearly out of control as she attempted to steady them.

 CHAPTER 11

"I don't feel well," she admitted to her mother during a short break in the history unit that afternoon.

Mom had been talking with two other students, slightly older than Heather. Two boys from their church were also homeschooled. Kevin was hanging around with them, deciding what essays to write. "A discussion on the balance of power would be great," one of the other boys suggested.

Kevin seemed to like the idea. Heather could tell by his wide, bright eyes. She, on the other hand, could scarcely stand up. She'd pushed herself this far through, but now felt so tired she just wanted to put her head down on the table and give in to sleep.

Mom looked at her over her glasses. "Are you ill or just tired?"

She wanted to say "both," but that wasn't true. Fact was,

she was dog tired. Her own fault. "I'm really wiped out," she said.

"Well, why don't you sit on the couch to do some reading?" Mom suggested.

What she really wanted was to go to her room and lie down there in the quiet. Why hadn't she gone to bed earlier last night? But she knew the answer. The truth was, she'd denied herself food and paid the price—much to the anger of her skating partner and older brother. How was she going to get down to nothing with Kevin hounding her?

She carried her books to the living room, as Mom recommended. Getting settled into the cushions, she knew right off this was a mistake. The sofa was far too comfortable, and the movement of her eyes on the page only served to make her sleepier. Almost before she knew it, she was sound asleep.

But in her dreams, she was light as a feather. She was also hungry, the empty feeling in her stomach exaggerated. As the dream progressed, she realized that she was beginning to get hooked on the hunger pangs. The feeling was actually enticing, something she liked. Somehow, though, she could sense that her family and friends, and even the Girls Only Club members, were afraid for her. But that, of course, was only in her dream.

When she awakened, the other kids had left. Mom, Joanne, and Tommy were doing an art project at the dining-room table. "Where's Kevin?" she asked.

"Lifting weights," said Mom. "Want to join him?"

"Too tired." She headed toward the stairs.

"School's not finished for the day," Mom said suddenly.

Returning, Heather asked, "What's next?"

It was clear that Mom was displeased. "Well, if you're too tired to do your schoolwork, then you must certainly be too tired to attend ballet class . . . and later, your Girls Only Club."

Mom was smart that way. She had her coming and going. Without saying more, Heather waited for her next assignment—a writing project—from her teacher-mother. She shouldn't have been too surprised at her own usually tenacious spirit. It was obvious she'd inherited persistence from Guess Who.

Heather yanked on the locker-room door at Natalie's Ballet School. Rushing inside, she was eager to get ballet class over for the day. Livvy and the other girls were already dressed and chattering at one of the mirrors, looking at something posted on the wall.

She couldn't care less. Not the way she felt at the moment. She wandered over to her own small locker, worked the combination lock, and pulled it open. Inside the locker door, smiling Russian ice dancers taunted her. Yet she knew better than to feel upset about the poster. After all, she'd searched high and low for the fantastic picture of ice dancers Pasha Grishuk and Evgeny Platov. She knew the grueling schedule and dietary provisions these superior skaters certainly must have adhered to, to get what they wanted. To reach their goals and dreams.

She found herself staring at them, wishing she could speak their language. Wishing she could get a grip on her life as a great skater . . .

Just then, Jenna and Manda came dashing over to her. "Have you heard?" Jenna said.

Still almost in a daze, she turned slowly. "Heard what?"

"Newman's department store is hosting a modeling agency," Jenna said.

Manda's eyes were absolutely twinkling. "They're interviewing prospective models next Wednesday."

Livvy wandered over to join them. "Yeah, but it's too bad."

"What do you mean?" asked Heather.

"None of us has any extra time," Livvy said glumly.

Jenna nodded, too, as if reality were sinking in. "True."

"Wait a minute," Heather said. "How'd you hear about this?"

Manda pointed to the poster near the mirror, across the locker room. "Check it out for yourself."

"I will!" And she charged off, feeling an unexpected surge of energy.

She scanned the ad with her eyes. It was *very* interesting. She read every word carefully. There were going to be agency directors flying in from New York City next week. They would look at portfolios—*no problem*, she thought—as well as narrow down the number of contestants. Whoever made the final cut was offered a modeling contract.

"Is it runway modeling, commercial, or catalogs?" she asked the others.

"Probably any of that, if you're good enough," Jenna said. "But it clearly says they train you, teach you everything you need to know. Even set up appointments for your work."

"But only if you have the look they want," Manda added. *The look* . . .

She wondered what that might be. If they meant the hollowed-out look, like the young models in her teen magazine at home, she thought she could pull *that* off by Wednesday. Less than a week away, she could maybe do it if she went without eating between now and then. Yes, that's what she'd do.

"I think I'll show up and see what it's all about," she said.

Livvy wrinkled up her nose. "You're kidding, right?"

She whirled around, bending and limbering up. "This is just what I've been waiting for."

Jenna and Manda exchanged glances. "How come you've never said anything to us about modeling before?" Jenna asked.

"Maybe you weren't listening."

"But we hang at Girls Only together and never once have you said anything." Jenna was unwavering.

"Guess I don't say everything I'm thinking." Heather shrugged it off.

Livvy frowned. "What about your summer ice event,

Heather? How will you place there if you're attending modeling classes or whatever?"

"Not *classes*." She spun around. "Didn't you read the ad? They find you *work*."

Manda joined her in bending and warming up. "I'd rather keep focused on one thing at a time. Life gets less complicated that way."

"Yeah, one thing at a time," Jenna echoed.

Livvy suggested they go to the barre and get ready for class. "Modeling's not for me, I can tell you that right now."

Heather was surprised—that comment coming from beautiful Livvy. "How will you know if you don't try out?"

Livvy shook her head. "I don't have the look they want, I'm sure of it."

Jenna grinned. "But maybe Heather does."

Heather wondered what Jenna meant by that. "Which means?"

"It's just that you're so tiny . . . the way they like models to be," Jenna replied.

Heather knew she probably wasn't even close to being tall enough. Models that made it big were usually close to six feet tall. Never much shorter. There was no chance she'd grow that much in a few days.

"Personally, I think it's silly," Manda said.

Think what you want, Heather decided.

"The four of us have athletic goals, in case you forgot," Jenna joined in the chorus.

"Who said anything about giving up goals?" she asked.

Jenna shot her a weird look. "Well, what will Kevin say?"

She should've known that was coming. Her girl friends always cared too much about what Kevin thought about everything. "My brother has nothing to say about it."

"But he's the other half of your skating partnership," Livvy said softly. "Doesn't that count for something?"

Of course it counted. She knew it did. But Heather was feeling just stubborn enough to stand firm in her quest. "Everyone, just back off."

"Fine," said Manda, pouting.

"It's time for ballet, besides," said Jenna, turning to go.

Livvy gave Heather a puzzled look but kept quiet.

When Natalie called for centerwork, Heather was glad. What did Manda, Jenna, and Livvy know about anything, anyway?

CHAPTER 12

At home, Heather stayed in the shower much longer than usual, trying to rinse away the memory of her girl friends' stinging remarks. So what if they weren't interested in showing up for the modeling try-outs. Who cared what *they* thought?

Lathering up for the second time, she remembered how outspoken Livvy had been. Livvy Hudson, typically sweet and considerate, had been downright direct. What had come over her? Was it that she was really interested but knew she couldn't honestly take on one more event in her week? Was that it? Or was there more to it?

Livvy and her father barely made ends meet sometimes. That was partly the reason for Livvy's grandmother coming to live with them. *"Out of necessity,"* Livvy had said early in the year.

Of course, Heather wouldn't be rude and bring up such a thing. But she suspected that to be the reason behind Livvy's disinterest. What else?

Manda and Jenna had been equally hostile. Well, maybe hostile was stating it a little strongly. But they *were* defensive. Drying her hair, Heather wondered why.

In her room, she chose a soft blue warm-up suit to wear to Jenna's house. Girls Only Club meetings were some of the best times of each week. It was fun to wear something comfortable. Sometimes, they worked together to come up with new ballet routines.

Today she was eager to see how many healthy recipes had been gathered since last Friday. Livvy's idea of a cookbook was really a terrific one. They could sell lots of copies at church and around the neighborhood. Another good place to market them was the homeschooling network in town. Mom knew all sorts of folks devoted to home teaching. Families who might appreciate a cool cookbook like theirs.

When she headed to the basement, Heather found Kevin playing with Tommy. "Where's Mom?" she asked.

"She ran an errand," Kevin said, looking up. "Where are you headed?"

"If it's Friday, it must be Girls Only," she taunted him.

"Oh yeah." There was a mischievous twinkle in his eye. "You're making a cookbook to raise money . . . for what?"

She wouldn't go there. It was a setup. She could see it on her brother's face. "Never mind."

He shook his head. "You know, it's kinda hard to overlook

something so completely ridiculous," he muttered. "You've quit eating, but you're putting together a cookbook. How does that make any sense?"

"Oh, what do *you* know?" she said under her breath.

He stood tall just then, grabbing Tommy and swinging him around the room. Tommy let out a few screams of delight. "Faster . . . swing me faster," their younger brother hollered.

"Stop it!" Heather shouted. "Just stop it."

Kevin slowed Tommy down and stopped. He frowned. "Relax, Heather. Nobody's out of control here."

No one except me, she thought.

Heather was the first to arrive at the Songs' home. Jenna Song was lying on her bed, talking to her furry feline, Sasha, high in her attic bedroom. The room was the largest bedroom Heather had seen in her life. When Jenna and her family moved to Alpine Lake last fall, they'd knocked out a wall in order to make the upstairs room a combination bedroom and ballet practice area. The only thing the room lacked was a hardwood floor for full-blown dances.

"Hey! You're early," Jenna said, spying her in the doorway. "Come in and relax."

Heather inched into the room, going to the corner near the window. "It's nice and quiet up here."

"Isn't it, though?" Jenna tickled her cat's nose.

Heather was silent, staring down at the rooftops of the other houses.

"Something on your mind?" asked Jenna.

"Oh, I don't know."

Jenna chuckled. "Well, if you don't . . . I sure don't."

Heather thought about that. Should she tell her friend about her nagging desire to be skin and bones? What would Jenna think?

"C'mon, Heather, talk to me." Jenna came over and sat on the floor across from her.

"You won't laugh?"

"Never."

She'd have to test the waters first. See if Jenna was the kind of friend she thought she was. "Bet you've never wanted to starve yourself skinny . . . have you?"

Jenna frowned, pulling on one side of her short hair. "Hey, I've heard all about eating disorders, if that's what you're talking about."

"I didn't say anything about disorders." Now she was stalled. Maybe talking to Jen wasn't such a good idea, after all.

"So what are you saying?" Jenna twisted first one side of her dark hair, then the other. Her deep brown eyes were very serious, like she was struggling to understand.

Heather pushed ahead, unsure of herself. "My brother thinks I'm fat."

Jenna laughed softly. "I doubt that."

"No, I'm serious. Kevin said I was too heavy one day during our practice."

Jenna sat with her knees under her chin. "Surely he was joking."

"I don't think so." She sighed. This was harder than she thought. "I want to be thin, Jen. Thinner than you are . . . thinner than I am now."

Frowning, Jenna looked at her. Really looked. "Hey, girl, you're starting to scare me. Am I hearing you right?"

Heather nodded. "I've never been more serious."

"So . . . what's it you're doing? Cutting out eating, is that it?"

"And I'm working out a lot."

"Working out? Like how much?" Jenna's eyes glistened.

"Several extra hours a day."

Jenna scrunched up her mouth. "Does your coach know?"

"Nobody knows but you." At last, she'd told someone. What would Jenna's reaction be?

"Wanna know what I think?" Jenna said softly, reaching out her hand.

"Sure."

"From everything I've heard and read—and, believe me, stuff like this gets around—you do *not* want to get caught up in the anorexic thing. I've seen girls my age get so high from the endorphins released during the starvation process, they actually get hooked on them. It's addictive." She scooted over next to Heather. "Please, don't even think of losing weight that way. It's dangerous."

She was frustrated at Jenna's reaction. "I don't get it. You think it's wrong not to eat?"

"Wrong and stupid, you pick. I've heard of some girls who'd rather cut off their arm than eat. They get sucked into the craving for the starvation high. Ten percent of them end up dead."

"Really? Dead?"

"Hey, if you don't eat, you die. Simple as that."

Heather hadn't thought of it quite that way. "You're sure about this?"

"My gymnastic coach could tell you a thing or two. That is, if you don't believe me."

She didn't know what to think. Jenna seemed so convincing. Sure of herself. And Jen ought to know this stuff, coming from the athletic world she, too, lived and breathed daily.

"Don't say anything to Livvy and Manda, okay?" she said, beginning to tremble.

"Well, I won't promise forever. I'm a better friend than that. If you need to control something in a major way, I would never suggest the food-less route."

They were silent for a moment. Then Heather whispered, "I'm sorry, Jen. I want to be skinny. I really do."

"And right now you're shaking. So how's that going to help you enjoy the club meeting in a few minutes?" Jenna's face was solemn. "When's the last time you ate?"

She wouldn't tell. That was her business. Her secret. Getting up, she went to the barre. "Sorry, Jen. Guess I made a mistake."

Jenna followed her over, staring at her in the mirror. "You're wrong about that. You did the right thing telling me. Because I refuse to let you get sucked into this dead end you're headed for."

Heather was nearly too weak to protest. But her silence was her best defense. So she said no more.

CHAPTER 13

Both Livvy and Manda arrived late to Girls Only. Heather really wished they'd shown up on time. Maybe then she wouldn't have blabbed her soul to Jenna. Now, someone else in the world knew what was going on in her head. And she wasn't so sure her gymnast friend would keep quiet about it.

"What recipes did you bring?" Livvy asked as the meeting had come to order.

Heather had carefully printed out the recipes she thought fit best under the High-Energy Snacks heading. She showed the Bars of Iron recipe first.

"Read off some of the ingredients," Jenna said.

She wasn't so sure she wanted to think about food, let alone read about it. But she did, for the sake of the club. "There are raisins and molasses in it."

Manda wrinkled up her nose at the molasses.

"Oats and ginger, too," Heather said. Just the sound of the word *raisins* made her mouth water. She was so hungry.

But no, she wouldn't think about it. Not now. Not with Jenna, Livvy, and Manda sitting here, staring at her with bright eyes and full stomachs. Nope, she'd stick it out as long as possible. At least until the modeling agency came to their little town.

They were in the middle of voting on a title for their cookbook when Jenna's mother knocked on the door. "Jenna, dear, can you watch your baby brother for me?"

Jenna glanced over her shoulder at the rest of the girls. "You don't mind, do you?" she asked the rest of the club members.

"No problem," Manda spoke up.

"We'll help you entertain him," Heather offered.

Livvy nodded her head, agreeing that they'd all pitch in and baby-sit. "It'll be fun."

Jenna left the room and returned with little Jonathan in her arms. The baby's olive skin tone matched Jenna's, and his eyes widened as he looked around at all of them. Then his face lit up with a big smile when he spotted Heather. "Aw, he's adorable," she said, getting up and going over to Jenna. "May I hold him?"

Jenna gave her the strangest look. "Are you strong enough?" Jen whispered.

She knew what Jen was getting at. "Well, maybe I . . ."

Jenna moved past her and went to sit on the floor with her baby brother. "He's crawling everywhere now," she said, setting him down in the middle of the floor.

Just then, the cat jumped down off the bed, and tiny Jonathan pointed at Sasha. "Oh," he said, crawling toward the furry creature.

"Watch this," Jenna said.

The girls were spellbound, watching Jonathan's every move. His cute little hands sprang out, and he began crawling toward the golden-haired cat. But Sasha only allowed the baby to get within inches of her. Then she skittered under the bed skirt to a safe hiding place.

Baby Jonathan just blinked his dark eyes, making sweet, high-pitched sounds.

"Does he talk?" Manda asked.

Jenna nodded. "He says 'Mama,' 'bye-bye,' 'hi,' and 'Dada.' "

"What's he call you?" asked Livvy.

Jenna smiled. "My brother only points at me and grunts."

"That's interesting," Heather said, observing the small child. She wondered what would happen if a baby didn't eat. How long before he or she would starve? Like the children on TV, in Third-World countries where every day babies die by the thousands.

Jenna's voice brought her out of her reverie. "Let's do our best to compile the recipes today. Then when we're ready, I'll make the cover. Unless someone else wants to."

"Go for it," Manda said.

"Yeah, you'll come up with a nice design," Livvy said.

"Use your computer program, maybe," suggested Heather. But her thoughts were on getting home, lying down. She felt so terribly weak.

Heather was glad Mom was out doing some shopping when she arrived home. Quickly, she slipped off to her bedroom, eager for a nap. But her rest was short-lived. Joanne knocked on her bedroom door, waking Heather.

"What do you want?" she asked.

Joanne poked her head inside. "Are you awake?"

"Not really."

"Kevin said to tell you that someone left a phone message for you, he thinks." Joanne's lips curled into a smile.

"What do you mean, 'he thinks'?"

Joanne stared back at her. "Just what I said."

She sat up in bed, groaning. "Will you just please tell me what you mean?"

"It's hard to hear who's on the voice mail," came the reply.

"So . . . it's still not fixed?"

"Better go listen," Joanne said. "Maybe you'll recognize the voice."

Why should I care?

Joanne stood there, like she was waiting for Heather to

get up and go to the phone. "Well, are you going?"

"Not now . . . I'm tired."

"And crabby," Joanne whispered.

But Heather had heard her sister. "Please close the door."

"You want me to leave?"

"Please." *The sooner the better*, she thought.

Taking her time, Joanne shut the door behind her. And Heather leaned back on her bed, closing her eyes. But now it was impossible to fall asleep again. She was too curious. Who had left the message? One of her friends from church, probably. Or maybe one of her Girls Only friends.

But she'd just been with Jenna, Livvy, and Manda. So . . . what would *they* want? The more she thought about it, the more she wondered, secretly, if Micky Waller had called.

"Micky wants to talk to you," Livvy had said on the phone the other day.

That got her up. She slipped down the hall to her parents' room and checked the voice mail. Joanne was right. It was almost impossible to hear who was talking. Almost.

Thank goodness she'd checked before Dad and Mom did. Yes, she was fairly sure it was Micky. But the number he'd left where he could be reached wasn't clear. At least he'd called. That was enough.

Feeling better just thinking about a boy calling her, she hurried downstairs. She opened the refrigerator and found a jar of peanut butter. She spread a small amount on two long stalks of celery and ate them both. She'd broken her fast, but the snack might curb her appetite for supper.

She headed downstairs to the family room, only to discover Kevin lifting weights in the corner of the room. "I'm next," she told him.

Kevin spouted back. "Since when do you just waltz in here and demand to be next?"

"Since right now."

He was silent. She'd made him angry. Not a good thing for either their working relationship or their brother-sister rapport. Neither one.

She waited her turn, wishing somehow they could clear the air between them. She wanted to improve their skating relationship especially. Fact was, she'd never forgiven him for dropping her.

"Did you get your phone message?" he asked when he was finally finished. On his way past her.

"Maybe."

He shook his head and left the room.

Eyeing the exercise equipment, she set the timer for one hour. Instead of doing homework, she was going to lift arm and leg weights for a solid sixty minutes. Since Mom was probably at the grocery store, she figured she would be fine with this. Nobody had to know.

She turned on the contemporary Christian station—one in Colorado Springs—that made its way to Alpine Lake. She was glad they got the station, because the town was too small to support its own major stations.

So she worked out, hard as she could, the upbeat music and her own thoughts filling her mind.

CHAPTER 14

On Monday, two days before the modeling agency came to town, Heather asked her mother if she could go and "try out."

"How are you going to fit everything into your life?" Mom asked.

She was ready for that question. "I can do it," she said. "I'll work even harder if I have to."

"Well, how do we know these folks are legitimate?"

"Call Natalie Johnston. Do you think Natalie would advertise something that wasn't on the level?"

Mom glanced toward the ceiling. "Seems to me, your father and I will have to check things out. *If* you go at all."

"Oh please, Mom, won't you come with me? Ask whatever questions you want to, just let me interview." She was starting to feel desperate.

Mom sat her down in the living room. "Honey . . . can you tell me, is this the reason you've quit eating?"

She looked away. "I haven't quit, not completely," she said softly.

"Do you want to be a model more than anything else?" asked Mom.

"Not more than skating, but I *do* want to see if I have a chance."

Mom touched her hand. "You haven't been yourself for over a week, Heather. I want to help you."

She remembered hearing her mother's prayer last week—the night she'd crept to the kitchen for some crackers and milk. She knew her mother was concerned, but there was no need. "I don't need help, Mom."

"I think you do. And I've made an appointment with the doctor." The corners of Mom's eyes were glistening. "Tomorrow, after lunch, we'll go together."

She knew there was no talking Mom out of this. She was determined; motivated by what, Heather didn't know.

"I'm not sick," she said, making an effort. "I don't need a doctor."

"Well, he can check on your knee, at least." Mom got up and reached for Heather. "I love you, kiddo. You're going to be just fine."

Just fine . . .

How did her mother know? Did she have any idea what was going on? Did she?

Before supper, the phone rang. Fortunately, Heather answered on the second ring. "Bock residence."

"Heather . . . is that you?"

Her heart skipped a beat. "Yes, and who's this?"

"It's Micky Waller. Remember, we talked at the mall rink last week?"

Sure, she remembered. How could she forget? "Hi, Micky. How's it going?"

"I called you before, but your voice mail sounded strange."

"It was, but it's fixed now," she told him, not sure what else to say.

"That's cool."

There was a long, awkward pause. Heather didn't know if she should speak first or if Micky should. She felt terribly tense. Was this how it was when a boy called a girl? They hardly knew what to say to each other?

At last, he said, "I saw an ad for a modeling agency at Natalie Johnston's studio."

"Really? I saw it, too."

"So . . . are you going to try out?" he asked.

"I might."

"Hey, really? Well, guess what? I'm going over there, too." He went on to say that he heard the agency was looking for kids, boys, girls, and older people.

"You're kidding, it's not just for girls?" she asked.

"No, and they offer commercial, runway, and catalog opportunities," he said. "My dad called the phone number listed on the ad. They actually get you set up for a portfolio and slides and everything."

"For how much?"

"I think it's six hundred dollars."

"That much?" she said.

"Seems like a lot, but if you make the final, *final* cut, they'll make appointments with different modeling companies for you. It's great."

She wondered if Micky was planning a future in skating. But she didn't ask. She didn't care, not really. Her interest in Micky was purely shallow. She thought he was nice, of course—and cute—but she didn't have time for a close friendship with a boy. Not at her age.

"Well, thanks for the info," she said, thinking she ought to get going.

"Uh, sure. Can I call you again?"

"You know what? It might be better if we just talk to each other at the rink sometimes. I'm *so* busy with training and my homework." She told him she was homeschooled, too. "We have lots of hours and requirements to meet for the state of Colorado."

"That kind of study is real tough, isn't it?"

"We like it that way. No time wasted, you know."

They said their good-byes, and by the time the conversation was over, Heather felt she knew Micky much better than before. But most of all, she was surprised that the agency was accepting *boys*.

Their family doctor seemed almost too pleased to have her visit. "Let's see how that knee's healing," he said, poking and prodding at it. She walked down the hall and up, turned her feet inside and out for him. Even twirled on the carpet to show him how "just fine" her knee was.

But the one-on-one conversation she had with the doctor—Mom outside, in the waiting room—was the most painful. "Your mother tells me you haven't been eating much lately," he began.

She nodded.

"Are you not feeling well these days, Heather?"

"Oh, I'm fine."

"I see." He folded his arms across his chest, studying her through his glasses. "Still have a good appetite?"

"Yes."

"Just aren't eating?"

"Yes."

"And can you tell me why that is?" He tilted his head the way her father often did when he was probing for answers.

"Well, I want to look skinny . . . uh, thin."

"According to our charts, you're quite slender, just as you are."

"But I want to be thinner."

"Is there any particular reason why?"

She chuckled slightly under her breath. Doc wasn't going to hear about Kevin today. Nobody needed to know how angry she was at him. "I skate lots better when I feel light, that's all."

"Yes, I suppose you do," he replied, getting up and going to the table. He brought back with him a small model of a human skeleton. "Have you ever seen one of these?"

"Only here, in your office."

"Do you understand that there are many aspects to our bodies?" He paused. "Our bones need certain foods in order to maintain health." He continued on, reciting the importance of tissue, muscles, and nerves. "All essential to hold us together." Here, he smiled at her. "We need food to recharge our human machine."

He wasn't telling her anything new.

"Any questions?" he asked.

"No."

"All right, then I'll see you back again next week."

Next week?

"I'm coming back so soon?" She didn't get it.

"Each week, we'll talk . . . okay with you?"

She was still baffled. This was a first. Something Mom had dreamed up, or what?

Before she left, the nurse weighed her and measured her height, recording it in a book.

Very weird, she thought.

CHAPTER 15

By some miracle, Heather's parents consented to allow her to try out with the modeling agency. Mom accompanied her, arriving a half hour before the place actually opened.

They sat in the car, chatting calmly. Mom wasn't pushy, even though she had every right to be. Yet Heather could hardly wait to go through the process of being chosen or not.

By the time the doors opened, at least fifty people had gathered. Even several men and women. But mostly girls her age had come, along with several boys. A few small children were present with their mothers, too.

First thing, she was asked to fill out a questionnaire, asking her vital statistics: chest, waist, and hip measurements. Along with that, her height and weight. She knew her weight and height precisely because she had been weighed at the doctor's office yesterday. *One hundred and two pounds . . . five feet four inches*. She'd lost three pounds in almost two weeks. Not bad.

When her name was called, two women, beautifully dressed and made up, looked her over, starting with her face. She was also asked to show her hands. "Do you have any scars or tattoos?" one asked her.

"None."

She noticed that most of the girls were at least five feet six inches or taller. She was one of the shortest girls in her age group. Also, one of the thinnest.

"Please have a seat, Miss Heather Bock," one of the women judges said.

Miss Heather Bock. Had a nice ring to it, she decided.

Heather and her mother waited together until the next group of contestants was called. "Do you think I'll make the first cut?" she asked her mother, crossing her legs at the ankles and sliding them under the chair.

"Oh, honey, I'm sure you will." Mom seemed so confident, so poised. Just the way Heather wanted to be. "But if not, please don't take this hard. It's just two women's opinions."

She knew what Mom was getting at. Still, she wanted to be chosen so badly.

"Always remember that what God thinks of you is what truly counts. You don't have to prove anything to your heavenly Father."

"I know, Mom." Yet Heather fought it. More than anything, she wanted to be accepted here on earth. By friends and family. By her skating partner.

"Promise you won't be upset if you don't make the final cut?" Mom was saying.

"But . . . what if I do? What then?"

"We'll talk about it if that does, indeed, happen."

"So I might be able to do some modeling in my free time?" she asked.

"We'll see."

She had a strange feeling her mother knew something she didn't. But she wasn't bailing out yet. She was going to hold her breath for this.

At long last, the names of girls in her age category were called. The names were called alphabetically. Her name was the fourth on the list!

"What'll I do now?" she whispered.

"Follow instructions, dear." Mom waited while Heather was asked to walk up and down a long aisle, with folding chairs set up on either side.

She felt very much like she did when she was skating. Gliding was more like it. She knew how to put one leg in front of the other, point her feet, and move gracefully.

"Thanks, Miss Bock," the woman said. "Can you and your mother return this evening?"

"Yes, I believe we can."

"At that time, we'll give you additional information about our company, how long we've been in business . . . that sort of thing. We can't guarantee any certain type of job, be it runway or catalog."

"That's fine," she said. "Thank you."

She could hardly keep from dashing back to the area where Mom sat. "I made it! They want me," she said. "Can you believe this is happening?"

Mom smiled and gave her a big hug. "Honey, I know how beautiful you are. No, I'm not a bit surprised."

Joanne and Tommy were surprised, though. And impressed. They trotted around behind her at home all afternoon. "Make way for Queen Heather," Joanne kept saying.

"I'll hold the edge of your royal robe," Tommy said.

"And *I'll* make her crown!" declared Joanne.

"Will you two cut it out," Heather said. "Mom, make them stop!"

Mom did her best, but when they were supposed to be working on social studies at the table, Joanne kept whispering, "Your Majesty . . ."

"Quit it," she whispered back. "I can't concentrate on my work."

Kevin sat at the opposite end of the table. "You've got it coming, Heather," he said.

"Meaning what?" she demanded.

"You know." But he refused to explain.

Heather told herself she really didn't care at all. Let him

say what he wanted. Truth was, *he* was the problem.

"Are we going back tonight?" Heather asked before supper.

"Maybe you and I will go together," Mom said. "You know how Dad feels about skipping church on Wednesday nights."

"Oh, that's right." She hadn't even remembered.

"How do you feel about being chosen?" Mom asked.

"Fine, if Joanne and Tommy would settle down about it."

Mom nodded, turning to open the cupboard, reaching for five plates. "I think you should have a long talk with Kevin before you decide about modeling, though."

"Why?"

"Kevin's future is on the line if you become distracted with something other than skating."

She'd gotten so caught up in her own interests, she hadn't even thought of Kevin. Or how any of this would affect him. "Do I *have* to talk to him?"

"Kevin's the other half of your ice-dancing partnership," Mom said. "You'll have to deal with him first."

She took a deep breath, not looking forward to discussing things with her older brother. "I'll be in my room," she told Mom.

"Heather?" Mom called after her.

She turned to see Mom standing with her apron on,

holding the dishes and the paper napkins. "Have you prayed about any of this?"

"Not really."

"Well, honey, will you?" Mom's last effort.

"Sure," she said. "I'll pray."

What could it hurt?

CHAPTER 16

They want me, she thought, standing at her bedroom window, looking out. She honestly believed that her plan to boycott eating, losing the few extra pounds, was the real reason she had been picked.

"I have the look," she whispered to the sky.

The sun was setting over the mountains, casting a purplish glow over the snow-scattered lawn and trees. She leaned on the windowsill and wondered how things might've turned out if she hadn't gone on the crash diet. Would she have been thin enough?

Mom wants me to pray, she thought. Yet inside, she felt proud of her personal accomplishments. So what if Kevin didn't approve. She could fit everything into her schedule. She knew she could.

What she really wanted to do was phone Livvy, tell her

the good news. But she'd told her mother she was coming to her room to talk to God.

Standing in the window while the sun shed its daytime duties, giving in to the twilight, she began to pray. "Dear Lord, since you know me so well, I'm sure you must know how *really* excited I am right now. It's so amazing to be chosen like this."

She paused, recalling how her dad liked to hear of her achievements, about the events of her day. She continued praying, picturing her heavenly Father listening intently, his eyes on her, wanting to share in her happiness. "I want to be . . ." Stopping, she felt suddenly sad. "I guess I ought to say that I want to be like you, God. But the truth is, I want my own way. I'm stubborn. And Kevin made me so mad when he dropped me and said . . . he said I was too heavy. I know that's not true. How could he say something so stupid?"

She sat down on the floor and cried. "I'm sorry, Lord. I had to do things my way. It was always about me . . . never about you." She brushed the tears away. "Forgive me for being such a jerk to my brother. For . . . depriving myself of food, just because I was so angry, so determined. And so wrong."

Her heart opened wide to God, and she stayed there in the stillness long after she had said "Amen."

Kevin seemed surprised to see her when she went downstairs to the family room. Sure enough, he was lifting weights. Probably so he could lift *her* and feel strong and poised on the ice.

"I'll be out of here in a minute," he mumbled.

"That's okay, take your time." She switched on the treadmill, setting it on one of the slowest settings. She would wait him out. Talk to him when he was finished huffing and puffing and stopped perspiring all over the place.

"So . . . when do you start your modeling work?" he asked.

"I'm not."

"But I thought—"

"When you're finished working out, we'll talk." She continued walking at a snail's pace on the treadmill.

Upstairs, something wonderful was simmering on the stove. The smells from the kitchen were wafting down, tantalizing her as she breathed steadily, not overdoing it.

"I'm finished now." Kevin was standing in front of her. "So talk."

She looked at her brother. Almost a mirror image of herself. *My dear brother and partner*, she thought.

"I'm sorry," she blurted. "I was stupid."

"So was I," he said.

"What?"

His face was serious, almost sad. "I think I started this whole mess, didn't I . . . about you not eating?"

"Don't blame yourself," she said quickly.

"Well, I do." He leaned his head against her forehead. "We have to work harder at considering each other's feelings."

"From now on," she promised.

"Me too."

"Race you upstairs?" she said, daring him.

"Bet I can eat more supper than you," Kevin teased.

"Bet you can't."

Joanne was setting the table when Heather came into the dining room. "I've been borrowing your body books," the younger girl confessed.

"So you're admitting it . . . you've been hanging out in my room, after all?"

"Just *borrowing*, that's all." Joanne was determined, it seemed, not to be called a liar.

"Why didn't you ask me?" She placed the napkins under the forks on the left.

"Didn't feel like it." Joanne cast an I-dare-you-to-yell-at-me look.

She waited for Joanne to finish with the knives and spoons. "Does this mean you're keeping your nose out of my stuff?"

"Maybe."

"You'd better."

Joanne grinned up at her. "Guess if you can forgive

Kevin, you can forgive me, too."

She hugged her bold little sister. "Yeah, I guess so."

Mom laughed till she cried when Heather told her the news. "I think I'd rather go to church tonight."

"You're going to skip the modeling meeting?" Joanne said, twirling around in the kitchen.

"I sure am." She couldn't help but smile. And Kevin was grinning right along with her. "Tomorrow, I need to get my hair trimmed at Dottie's Boutique," she said, heading for the dining room.

"How come?" Joanne asked.

"Makes me feel lighter." Getting her hair trimmed up always did that for her. It sure beat starving herself. "Do I have time to make a phone call before supper?" she asked Mom.

"Make it quick."

She hurried to the telephone and dialed Jenna's number. "I've got some good news for you."

"Let me guess," Jenna said. "It's about the modeling agency?"

"Sort of." She wouldn't make Jenna guess anymore. She told her the *real* news. "I won't be poking around at my food anymore. Doc says if I get back up to one hundred and five pounds, I'll be about right for my frame and build."

"You're photo perfect, Heather."

"Thanks," she said, believing it.

"Any time."

"I made the final cut with the modeling agency," she told her. "But I've decided you were right. I want to focus on ice dancing for now. Skating . . . and good health."

Heather wondered what was keeping Mom in the kitchen. She could hardly wait to say good-bye to Jenna and find out.

"The food smells so good," she told Mom.

Her mother smiled and dished up the baked potatoes. "Glad to hear it."

Heather carried the large bowl into the dining room. "Everybody, come and get it," she called, the first to be seated at the table.

After the prayer, Mom announced, "We're *all* going to church tonight."

Dad seemed to catch on without probing. His eyes smiled at the corners as he reached for his napkin.

"But first we're *all* going to eat supper," Heather said, picking up her fork. Her pin-thin days were definitely past.

Also by Beverly Lewis

PICTURE BOOKS

Cows in the House   Annika's Secret Wish

THE CUL-DE-SAC KIDS
Children's Fiction

The Double Dabble Surprise	Tarantula Toes
The Chicken Pox Panic	Green Gravy
The Crazy Christmas Angel Mystery	Backyard Bandit Mystery
No Grown-ups Allowed	Tree House Trouble
Frog Power	The Creepy Sleep-Over
The Mystery of Case D. Luc	The Great TV Turn-Off
The Stinky Sneakers Mystery	Piggy Party
Pickle Pizza	The Granny Game
Mailbox Mania	Mystery Mutt
The Mudhole Mystery	Big Bad Beans
Fiddlesticks	The Upside-Down Day
The Crabby Cat Caper	The Midnight Mystery

SUMMERHILL SECRETS
Youth Fiction

Whispers Down the Lane	House of Secrets
Secret in the Willows	Echoes in the Wind
Catch a Falling Star	Hide Behind the Moon
Night of the Fireflies	Windows on the Hill
A Cry in the Dark	Shadows Beyond the Gate

THE HERITAGE OF LANCASTER COUNTY
Adult Fiction

The Shunning   The Confession

The Reckoning

OTHER ADULT FICTION

The Postcard

The Crossroad

The Redemption of Sarah Cain

Sanctuary*

The Sunroom

*with David Lewis

MANDIE® Books

from *Lois Gladys Leppard* and
BETHANY HOUSE PUBLISHERS